Things My Daddy and 'Nim Taught Me...

30 Sayin's that shaped a culture

Bob-e Simpson Epps

Sayin's

ISBN: 978-0998776620

Printed in the United States of America.

Introduction

Things Daddy and 'nim taught me is not just a book. Rather it is the assembling of wisdom. Each of the wise sayin's or colloquialisms are filled with life lessons. What you will read are words that helped guide, shape and inspire me. Words that I began hearing as a young child. Words that stuck with me, challenged me, and held me accountable to myself and others.

I remember hearing both my dad and my mother making short statements that were laden with meaning. It was at the tender age of five that daddy made a statement and it stopped me in my tracks. It was filled with a brief description of how people show up. And, as it were I had to ask myself was I one of the people.

Wisdom can come in many forms, but it is up to each one of us to grab it, massage it, use it and accept the gift. I remember so clearly having time with my father as we sat on the porch and talked. It was in those moments that he would be in conversation and a sayin' would come forth. I began remembering the sayings that were shared and using them myself. After a while they found their place in my being and in my spirit. They flow freely out of my mouth.

It has always been a dream of mine to share the wisdom of my father, mother, and the elders who have been in my life with the world. The life lessons are as necessary today as they were in the past. So much of what is in this book is a part of what elders share in the hopes that their wisdom is given as a gift to the world and that someone is listening and living it out.

The sayin's transcend age, race, culture, geography and much more. Each can be used to teach life lessons, develop strategies for change, open ways of thinking and being and aide in the dialogue necessary to really see and hear someone else. You will find yourself smiling, laughing, maybe crying but certainly looking at life through a different set of lenses.

1

*"You know
where you been,
but you don't know
where you goin'."*

He sat looking out the window. It was a magical fall day. There was a bite in the air, yet the sun's rays offered more than a spectrum of heat. The leaves on the ground were piling up, but there weren't enough to get up with so many more on the trees. The walnuts would be gathered later. The produce from the summer gardens filled the freezers.

There was a time when he was sitting in a house he could never own, making 50 cents a day to feed, clothe, and care for his family. He would have been raking leaves and digging potatoes at that house he could never own on land his ancestors labored on until death befriended them. Today, he looked out the window, which he owned, and knew someone would be coming to rake and bag the leaves on the land he owned. He could look in any one of three deep freezers and decide what to eat.

Questions to Consider

When you are in a space, what comes to your mind?

Do you feel a sense of belonging?

If yes, what is it that makes you feel as if you are welcomed? If no, what makes you feel unwelcomed?

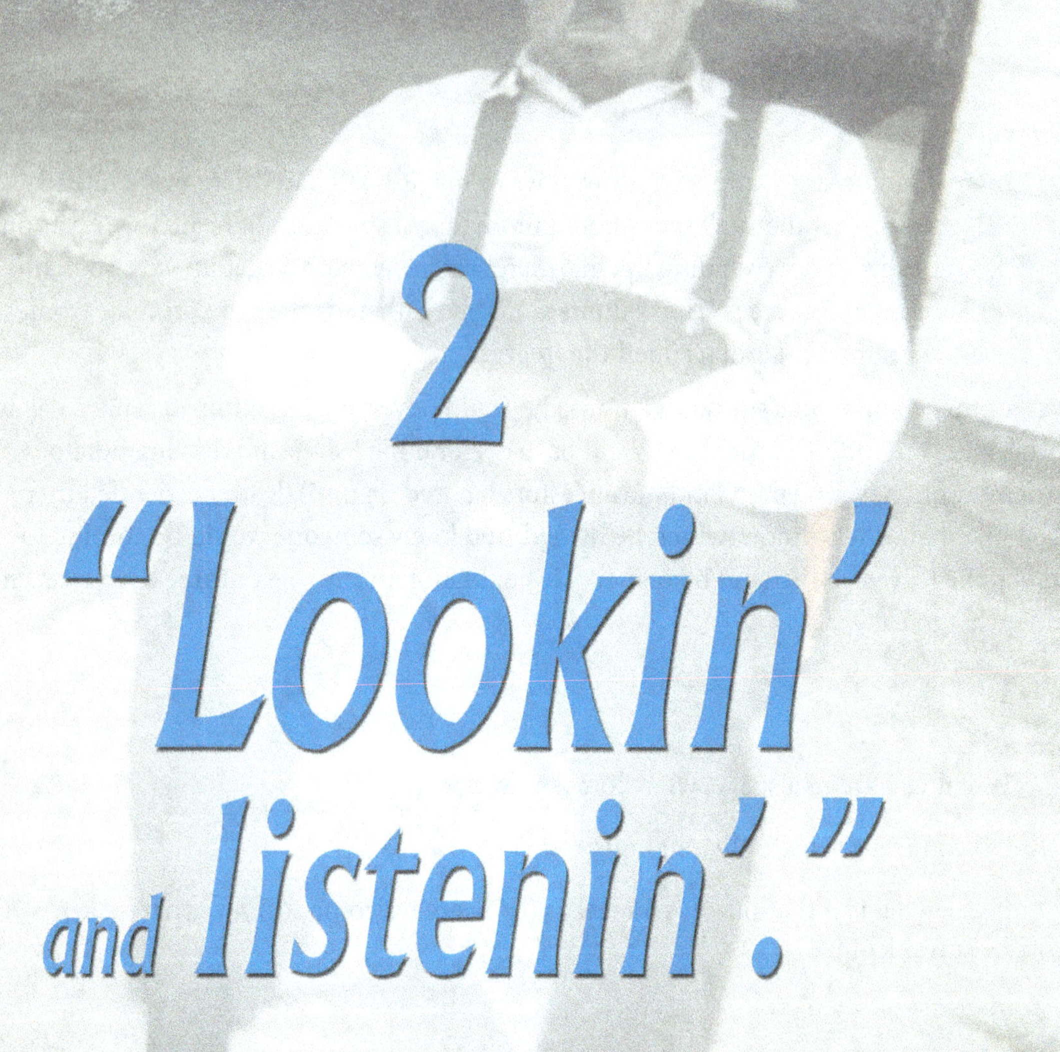

2

"Lookin' and listenin'."

The sun would soon be rising to greet him with a warm hello as he sat quietly on the porch. It seemed he always woke about 5:30 AM. Sitting in the same chair he had sat in for years was comforting but not comfortable; yet when he sat down, the cushions wrapped around, embraced, and cuddled him. The usual sounds of the small town called to him. He heard the morning mist settle in for the day. The flowers gently swayed as if yawning to open up to a new day. The grass and the trees displayed a bright, lush green with panoramic hues of color. All seemed well with the crickets, beetles, and birds as if they were softly saying, "I am here." In the background was the hum of cars and the sounds of voices.

Time passed as he watched one neighbor and then another, one small-business owner and then another, open curtains, unlock doors, and start their day. He sat and took it all in, never speaking or shouting a hello, but tentatively taking in the joyous birth of a new day, much the same as yesterday. But he knew it would be different than the day before.

Questions to Consider

How do you engage with the world?

Is humility anything you have ever thought about?

When you are in a new place/setting/environment, what is the first thing you look for?

3

"It's a long road that don't come to an end."

She sat in the meeting she called to discuss the Sixth Sigma Black Belt initiative she was leading. The results were much better than projected. The interdepartmental teams had finally begun to work together, with each assigning the right person to do the job. Each of the ten people around the table brought a unique style, talent, and persona to the whole. She had led the project amidst a lot of pain and anguish. Yet again, when she spoke, she only received a look—a five-second pause in the discussion, no acknowledgement—and the conversation took off again. She dug the heel of her right pump into the top of her left foot to acknowledge that she was indeed there, alive, breathing, and confident in her role.

Was today the day, or could she wait again until tomorrow?

Questions to Consider

Who might this person have been?

Who might have been the others in the room?

Have you experienced this? Have you witnessed this? Have you done this?

What would you, or could you, have done?

4

*"It's bad to have two faces,
It'll get you into trouble.
It's best to have a pleasant face
and not an ugly double."*

It was that time again when everyone would be trying out for a role in the Christmas concert. The lead singing roles for two of the most popular songs were going to be open. Having taken voice lessons for the past five years, she knew she was a cinch for at least one of the songs. Getting to the tryout early would give her a chance to do some voice exercises and some breathing and range practicing. She didn't see any cars in the parking lot and was sure she would have time.

Quietly, she walked down the hall to the choir room. She heard voices. It was Jolene and Helen. They were all like sisters and had just left her house after a three-day weekend. They had been in choir together since they were three years old. She stopped suddenly when she heard their conversation.

"She thinks she can outsing anyone in the alto section, tenor section, and even the soprano section."

"I know. I am so tired of hearing her singing every Sunday at church and every Monday and Wednesday in choir."

"Do you think she knows people like her and think she's good, but she's no Jill Scott?"

"Honey, if she knows, you wouldn't know it."

Of course, they couldn't be talking about her. She always honored requests to sing, but she never interjected herself or tried to be up front and center. It was the gift God had given her. She second-guessed herself and decided it couldn't be them as she strolled through the door.

Questions to Consider

What might have been your gut reaction if this had happened to you?

After more consideration, how would you handle this situation?

What are the values that shine through?

5

"Heap say,
but few do."

As she picked up apples in the lot next to her garden, Mr. Monroe called out how good her pies would be. Yes, those pound cakes, apple pies, and peach cobblers were always "slap yo' Mama good." Anything she touched was filled with melt delicious love. It was just that way; it caused everyone to fill their plates high and then do it again. The love she poured into her cooking was something.

He was one of the many who would be stopping by on Sunday to say hi and eat a few pieces of pie. He was one of the many who always said, "I'm gonna help you in the garden next summer." Well, she thought next summer had come.

Questions to Consider

What does it mean to be viewed as excellent?

When praise is offered with a promise that is not fulfilled, does it impact a relationship?

How might those who give praise step up in ways to offer support?

6

*"Doctor say, doctor do,
make yo' own potion
so you feel bran new!"*

She sat by the window waiting for the pain to go away. It was a combination of feeling downcast and having a headache that was dull and consistent and seemed to say, "You brought this on yourself." Yes, she'd gone out and pulled weeds and picked a few vegetables out of the garden. She was so grateful to have a garden. Getting fresh anything seemed to be impossible.

When she came in, she knew she would have to take something to begin feeling better. After looking in the medicine cabinet at over-the-counter remedies and the bottles of prescription drugs that had not served her well, she had almost given up. She called her mother and began to feel better after they spoke. The vegetables selected would marry well with the herbs and spices her mother and grandmother would bring.

Questions to Consider

Have you ever used other remedies to solve a problem?

What did you use, and what were the results?

Do you think it is important to look for new solutions to issues or challenges?

7

"Don't let yo' mouth
write a check

that yo' ___
cain't cash."

Yep, there was Tommy, standing in the middle of the pack, pushing an agenda that was his own. He was making promises and wanting folks to make a public commitment to what he was saying. I had made up my mind Tommy wasn't going to have the last word. I was stepping in and up. Yes, I was small in stature, but I felt big in my mind. This time I, Leon, was going to show them.

Okay, I said it. I had stepped up. It really felt good having my say. All the eyes were on me. Heads nodded, and some folks clapped and patted me on the back when I finished. I don't know what all I said. I spoke loud with passion, moving my hands and my body. I had studied Tommy and knew I could speak or perform in front of a crowd much better than he could. Yes, I, Leon, looked good and sounded good. It was such a rush of emotions and pride. Now I had to think of what I had said.

Questions to Consider

In what ways do you see yourself in Leon?

When you have overstated who you are or what you can do, did you correct it? If so, in what way(s)?

Is there a danger in not doing anything and just letting it go?

8

"Drive accordin' to yo' pocketbook."

My dad had gone with me to purchase my car. Yes, it was my first new car off of the lot. If felt really great to have him riding with me, a junior in college purchasing a new, not-used car! I must admit I really thought I was the sauce.

Aware that my dad was sitting in the passenger seat, I drove the speed limit as we talked. It was important not to show off. Daddy said, "Show me what it can do!" This was the moment I had been waiting for. I really wanted to go a bit faster. I pressed the gas, and the car went from 25 to 50 mph in a nanosecond!

Wow! This car was perfect for me. Then I heard the sirens but didn't think they were for me. I looked at Daddy, and he said, "Yeah, it'll take off, but you have to drive accordin' to yo' pocketbook."

Questions to Consider

Do you let other people influence you?

What have been some of the outcomes?

In hindsight, is there a response you might have to a person asking you to move in a direction you don't agree with?

9

"Take a little nothin'
and make
a whole lotta
somethin'."

They had all come for the family reunion, and tonight was the family dinner, recognition service, and dance at the Elks.

"What that girl doin'?"

"You just wait. She gon' show you somethin'."

Never having enough was something she was used to. With two small kids, her college tuition, and little money, inventions were always the answer to necessity. Down the steps she came. I would not have believed it if I had not seen it for myself. Only she could have pulled it off.

She had shown them the two small pieces of fabric she'd been saving. One was a half yard of striped fabric, and the other a yard of beautiful solid taffeta. As she sauntered down the steps, my mouth dropped. I saw what looked like the fabric she had. The outfit was pleated, tucked, and held together with four safety pins. She looked as if she had stepped out of *Vogue* magazine.

Questions to Consider

Do you believe scarcity can cripple you?

When was the last time you had to be creative to solve a problem/issue? What did you do?

10

"E'ry goodbye ain't gone."

George had been so good to me over the years. Because of him, I learned how to do my job and not just be good at it. I had become a leader in the field. I remember my first day of work. There were few people who even looked at me. I felt like a nothing in the middle of a whole lot of something. After all, I finished at the top of my class in high school, college, and graduate school. I was a scientist in a field that few people were in.

As an immigrant of mixed races, there were few places where I was accepted as being part of a community. With the passing of George, I felt totally lost. There was no one I felt connected to and comfortable with to ask questions and check my assumptions.

When I got a call from the prominent international leader, I didn't know what to expect. Fear seized me, and I was unable to speak. My brain said, "Say hello," but I was frozen. He then said, "George sent me a letter."

Questions to Consider

Have you experienced the loss of a friend, colleague, or family member and wondered what the future would hold?

In what ways did you keep going?

What memories of that person lie within you? What "rememberings" of that person have you shared with others?

11

"Some thangs' jes' don't take root."

Charles wanted desperately to go fishing with Uncle Dub. All his life, he had wanted to catch the big catfish. He had patiently saved his money and gotten the right fishing pole, the right line, the right hooks, and the right bait. *Shucks,* he thought, *I have been practicing my casting for months—well, years, truth be told.* Uncle Dub had tutored him, showing him what to do and the amount of force to use when casting.

Now standing on the banks, he was going to cast his line perfectly. Uncle Dub watched and said, "Go 'head." Poised and ready, Charles moved his head ever so slightly so the rising sun wouldn't be in his eyes. He planted his feet firmly and positioned his body, leaning back and rocking forward, holding the pole tightly as he cast. The agonizing scream paralyzed him. He looked over to see Uncle Ed dancing as the hook had sunk deep into his back pocket. "Uncle Dub, we practiced, and I did everything you told me! What went wrong?" he asked.

"Well, some thangs just don't take root," said Uncle Dub as he shook his head and laughed.

Questions to Consider

When was the last time you studied a subject or a process and tested it to see how well you would do?

How have you dealt with anything when you felt defeated?

What do you do, if anything, to deal with defeat?

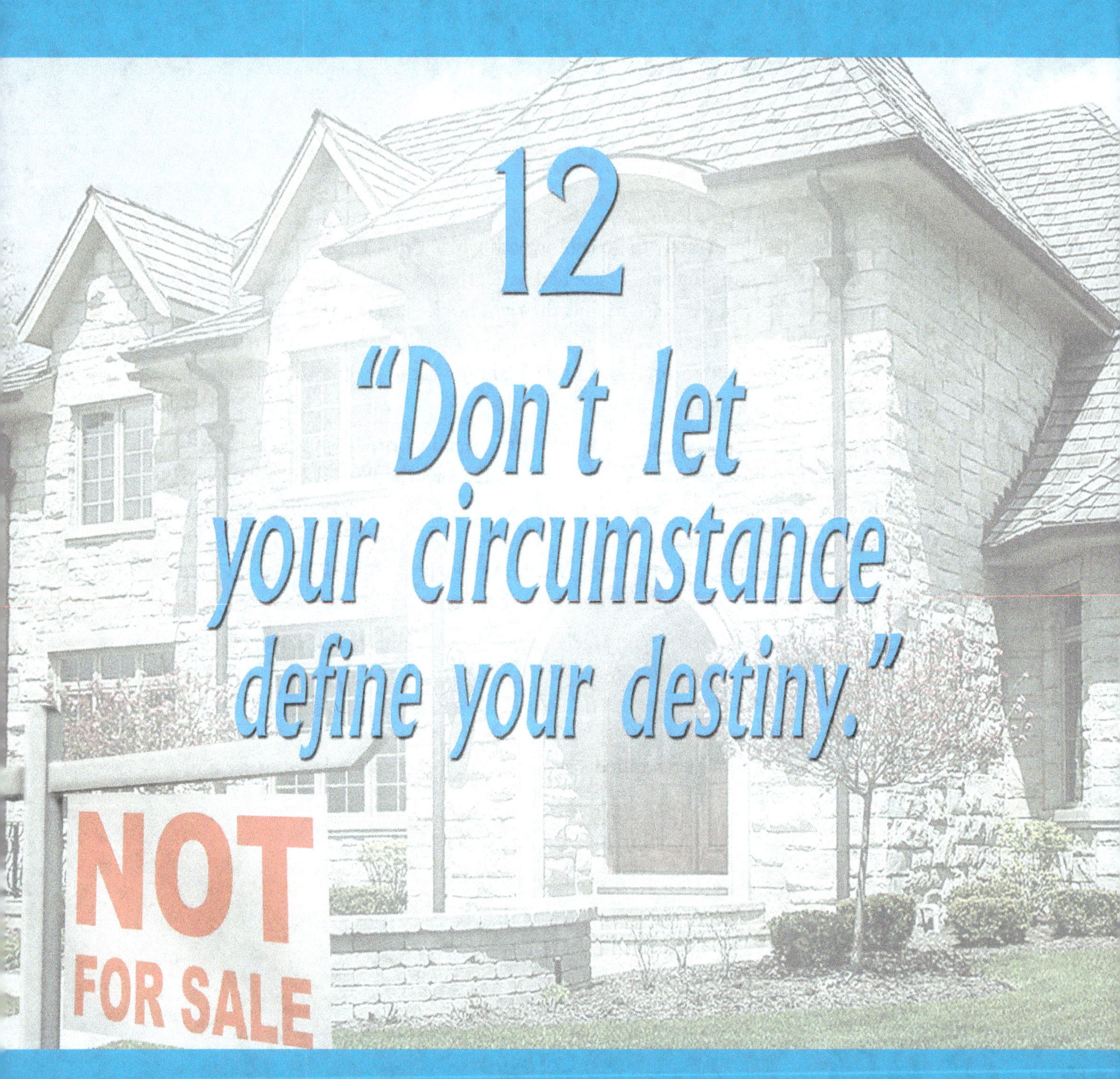
12
"Don't let
your circumstance
define your destiny."
NOT
FOR SALE

The notice had come too quickly. This was the first home he had purchased. As he left the meeting with the mortgage officer, he remained at a loss. What would he do? He had called all of the people the mortgage company had told him to call. He even called the federal government agencies of support found on the internet and waited for what seemed like hours to speak with someone. Each time, he'd been told to fill out a form or he was transferred to another party. What a dark period in his life. He sat motionless and stayed that way for the next week.

It was another sleepless night. He could hear the message as he opened his eyes and looked at the TV. He felt angry and wondered why they always show people across the country in such dire straits in the middle of the night.

As he dozed off, he saw a face that looked familiar, and the voice sounded like a childhood friend. It was Cathy. She looked fabulous, and she was standing tall. It couldn't be. She had been hit by a car at age nine and had always sat in a wheelchair propped up with pillows. Startled, he sat straight up in the bed. It was at that moment he decided he would not lose his home.

Questions to Consider

Have you ever felt hopeless? If so, what was going on?

If no, have you seen someone else who felt hopeless, and what did you think?

What conditions can shift hopelessness for you or for someone else?

13

"My back may be bent, but it ain't broke."

Retirement—now that's a joke. What in the world is a 60+ "supposed to be" successful person with an Enron, 9/11, Katrina setback to do? Moving to Minnesota had proven to be okay. The job with the state had not been what he wanted, but it was a job. He worked there and did well for two years. The benefits and lateral moves gave him a sense of security. He felt he would be able to grow and attain other jobs in the state system. Now it had been two years since he was told his job was being cut due to funding.

A walk around Lake Phalen was what he needed. He had been on one interview and then another. There had not been a single call for a second interview, let alone a job offer. The wife and kids had been real troopers as life slowly changed for them. No excess money meant no extras. He remained encouraged because he could use his truck, his tools, and his communication style to keep going until he got that call for an interview.

Questions to Consider

What keeps you going when things get tough?

How do you appreciate your strength when you are going through adversity?

Where do you go internally or externally when it seems as if there are no answers?

14
"E'rybody
got a spot
or a wrankle."

"Girl, did you hear about Shirley? I told Jean that hot-tail gal was gon' bring her plenty mouths to feed. I wouldn't have it."

This was always the conversation with Ms. Alice. According to her, all her children were angels. She constantly let everybody know how smart her daughter was.

Ms. Alice said, "My daughter Jessica may go out a lot, but she ain't brought no babies home." Jessica was Ms. Alice's oldest daughter. She went out a lot all right. She went with Joe the barber, Mr. Douglas the banker, and Rev. Jones—to name a few.

I thought to myself, *It ain't even worth bringin' up that the day would come when Ms. Alice would learn the truth. Jessica hadn't brought no babies, but it wasn't 'cause she wasn't workin' at it.*

Questions to Consider

Have you ever considered anyone as "the other" in a negative way?

What causes people to hold others accountable and not have that same accountability for themselves?

Do you ever look at yourself and consider ways to improve a shortcoming?

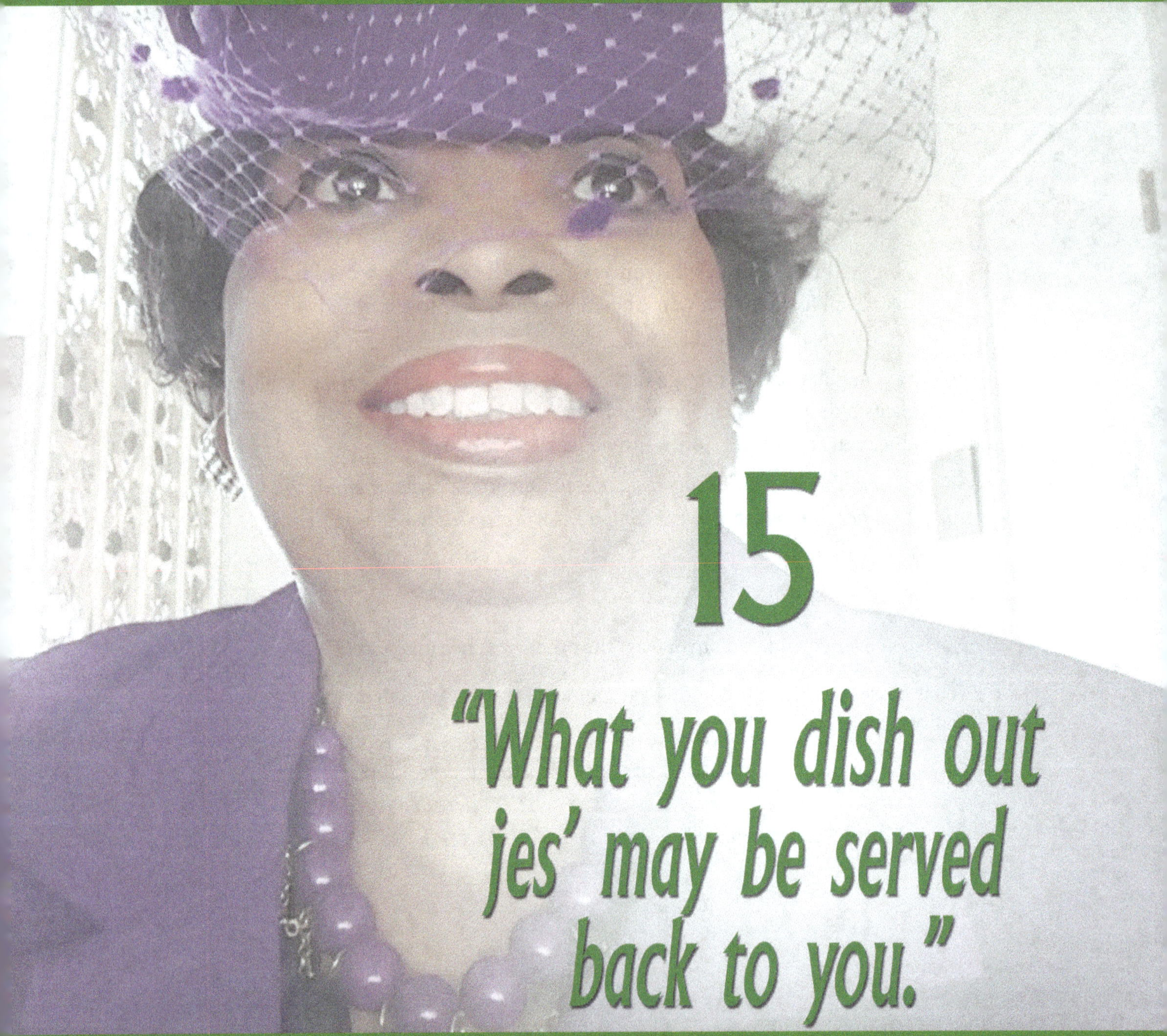

15

Yeah, Sister Margo had settled it once and for all! She didn't hesitate to let Deaconess Jamison know just how she felt. Who did this deaconess think she was deciding to do Women's Day a little differently? Especially since she had only joined the church three years ago. Sister Margo had been at the church for 30 years, and during all those years, they had always presented the first lady with a trophy. After all, Sister Margo started this years ago and knew it was the respectful thing to do then and still was.

Sister Margo had made her point and had gotten enough of the right folks to agree with her. On Women's Day, she walked up to the front of the church. As she moved to the front, all eyes were on her. She felt the admiration and respect she had built over the years. Everyone smiled, clapped, and greeted her just as they always had. She stood tall, pushed her shoulders back, and begin to speak as she took her rightful place. That happened a year ago.

It was Women's Day again. Now, the young women of the church stood up front and began recognizing one another. Sister Margo sat waiting to see if she or anyone else would be mentioned.

Questions to Consider

How important is it to keep things the same?

What does it feel like when you are leading the pack?

When shifts are made in your normal, how do you adjust?

16

"Ain't nothin' like bein' glad twice—
glad to see 'em come,
and glad to see 'em go."

"Aw Lawd, them folks comin' again."

"Yeah, and it will be good to see them."

Each time they came, there was so much fun. Mama would begin preparing right away. Everything had to be spotless inside the house and outside as well. She would have us mopping floors, putting clean linen on the beds, mowing the yard, sweeping the sidewalks, and putting out lawn chairs.

The kids were sweet and nice. They were shy and didn't talk much, but they would do anything you asked them to do. Daddy always enjoyed their dad. They would run around seeing the other men in the family, have drinks, eat, play bid whist, and tell some of the biggest tales you would ever hear. Some of the stories—well, most of the stories—always had one more thing added to it each time you heard it. Most of the time, the kids wet the bed; all of the time, they left guests, the kind that made you have to bomb your house and call Orkin. Yes, there was a lot to do once they left, but you did get to be glad twice!

Questions to Consider

When have you been excited about someone or something and it didn't measure up?

What did you learn from the experience?

Would you do it again? If yes, why? If no, why not?

17

"Clean as the board of health."

"Aw, sooky, sooky. Who that comin'?" Daddy asked. As we sat on the porch, we could see someone coming down 4th Street, walking with purpose, like they had somewhere to go. "My, my, my, he is really steppin'. Look like they wearin' all sky blue." This was the dialogue that usually occurred on a warm sunny Sunday morning. Watching people walk up and down the street was as interesting as seeing people drive around the block ten or more times. It was pitiful there was nothing to do. People overate, laughed too loud, had sex with whomever, and went to church. Seemed to me life here was a hot mess.

Wasn't long before Uncle Elbert was on the porch grinning.

"Hey, man, what you think? Clean, ain't I? I got blue shoes, blue socks, blue pants, blue shirt, blue vest, blue tie, blue coat, blue cuff links, blue hanche, and blue hat!"

Daddy laughed and said, "Yeah, man, you clean as the board of health." Daddy got to tell Uncle Elbert that at least two times per month and always on Sunday.

Questions to Consider

What stands out for you in the story?

Why does that stand out?

How does it reflect some quality or characteristic about you?

18

"*A little somethin'
better than
a whole lotta nothin'.* "

W ell, she knew she was qualified for both jobs. She had her eyes set on the higher-paying position. Going to school in another town became daunting. She knew a reliable car was important. School and a car cost more money than she had. Even with grants, scholarships, and the dreaded student loan, it was not enough.

As she walked out of the interview, her confidence was high. When she got home, the phone rang, and it was the company where she had interviewed.

"Did you get the job," Mama asked.

"Yes, I got the job, Mama, but it's only paying $1.55 an hour. I got to pay for school and my car."

"Well, how much was you makin' before you got the job?" Mama asked.

Questions to Consider

Have you ever experienced a time when you knew you were qualified for something and you didn't get it? If yes, what was it, and what did you do? If no, what do you think you would do?

Do you think taking something less is a statement about how you value yourself? If yes, why? If no, why not?

19

"Jes' keep livin'."

Grandma Jane saw her daughters out there playing and laughing, and she wondered who they would become as they grew older. Each had her own ways and personalities. Some had spirits that just leapt out at you. They didn't mind showing anyone who they were. But with each one, something special was always present. There was no need to wonder. They always laughed when she finished working around 2 PM. everyday. She showered, got dressed, did her hair and makeup, and sometimes even put on high heels.

With so many girls, she did her best to talk with them about taking care of themselves. Loving themselves enough was important for her to pass on. They thought it was all about Daddy coming home from work. That might have been part of it. She knew over time it would mean so much more as they began their life journey.

Questions to Consider

Do you recall anything you learned as a youngster that was silly or funny to you but you find yourself doing it today? If yes, what is it, and why are you doing it?

Is there a life lesson you want to pass on? What is it, and why do you think its important to pass on?

20

"A song ain't jes' words;
it's the rhythm, melody,
and cadence of yo' life."

Have you ever woken up and just had that feeling of overflowing joy? I love that feeling and reassurance of it being all right. Today was a beautiful Sunday morning. My sister Katherine insisted I go to church with her, and of course, I would sing. I had that Marvin Gaye, Luther Vandross type of voice. I loved traditional gospel music, but I always knew my lyrics were mine. Every time I sang in the choir, the words, melody, and movement elevated my mind and spirit. When I sang the solo part, I added in a few of my own lyrics. "Sing, Willie, sing!" Katherine, Sheila, and the whole church would erupt. My vanity was something else.

After singing, I'd sit on the pew, and there was an older lady in front of me who always said, "You better thank Him." She'd say this over and over again every time she was in church. Over the years, I've often thought about her. My yesterdays overlapping my todays. That saying "You better thank Him" resonates in my being. I understand the entire concept of thanking God for another day's journey. My path has had some falsettos, harmony, steady beats, and percussions that have taken in the melodies that come with living—and I thank Him.

Questions to Consider

What song or instrument would best describe your life to this point, and why?

If you could write a song about your now, what lyrics would you write?

What blend of instruments or types of music would you use, and why?

21
"Slick
to a can
of oil."

What a beautiful fall day! School had started again, and there was going to be a lot of fall dances to go to. The leaves made even the worst part of the city look beautiful. Martha Ann loved the gold, orange, and rust-colored leaves on the trees. Some of the trees still had a bit of green on them, which made the colors so vibrant! Some leaves even looked soft and velvety, depending on where the sun was in the sky. And, yes, she had put a different top in her school bag. It would look perfect on her, even if she had been warned.

As usual, her older sister had tried to tell her not to wear it. Martha Ann told herself older didn't mean smarter. As soon as she got to school, she slipped into the girl's bathroom. She couldn't wait to put on her secretly purchased pretty orange-ish gold blouse. When she tried it on at the store, she felt like the cream of the crop. Lilly had told her to leave it.

"Girl, you know our folks will have a fit, and I'm not letting you get me in trouble. Too much is showing," Lilly had said.

It had a little cleavage. Oh, well! With a smile on her face and a bounce in her step, she opened the door. There stood not just her sister but her mother as well.

Questions to Consider

When have you witnessed people doing something they knew they shouldn't be doing?

What did you tell them?

When have you thought about or did something and thought you had gotten away with it?

22
"Pissin' in high cotton."

I was elated to get the position as a global human resources manager. I didn't know what it meant. Of course, I knew there would be more people to support, cultures and languages to understand, time zones to adjust to, and highways and airways to travel. Now, after being in the role for more than two years, I felt the joy, sorrow, burden, and satisfaction of it.

Who would have thought a person who literally felt like a nothing could achieve this type of success? I sat looking out the window in a luxury hotel suite. I sat in my luxury bathrobe—which the hotel provided—sipping coffee, meditating, and watching dolphins swim. Who would have thought! I truly was in a space and a place of "who would have thought!" For today, I knew I had arrived! And I thought, *What y'all gon' do 'bout it?*

Questions to Consider

Do you understand what is being said in the story? How do you interpret it?

Reflect back on periods of your life journey when you were unsure and couldn't see your way?

Reflect on victorys you have had. How have you acknowledged them?

23

"Live so that yo' yesterday will make yo' tomorrow."

Being the first, she learned early that there was a lot she was expected to do. She went to school and fell head over heels in love with books. At six years of age, she was reading the maps and signs, helping her father navigate the highways as they drove to and from Mississippi. Every test she took, she received an A. When she got less than an A, she felt depleted. She'd kick herself and wonder what she was thinking to have missed an answer.

Yes, big sister Doty had loved to read. It paid off. She set the standard for many a person, not just her siblings, but others who are leaders in their family, community, places of worship, and professions. She was an example of "the apple not falling far from the tree."

Questions to Consider

Have you thought about what you do from day to day that is laying a sure foundation? If not, why not? If you are, what is one of the things you do? Where do you think it will lead you?

Do you feel social ills can have an impact on steps you are taking today for your future?

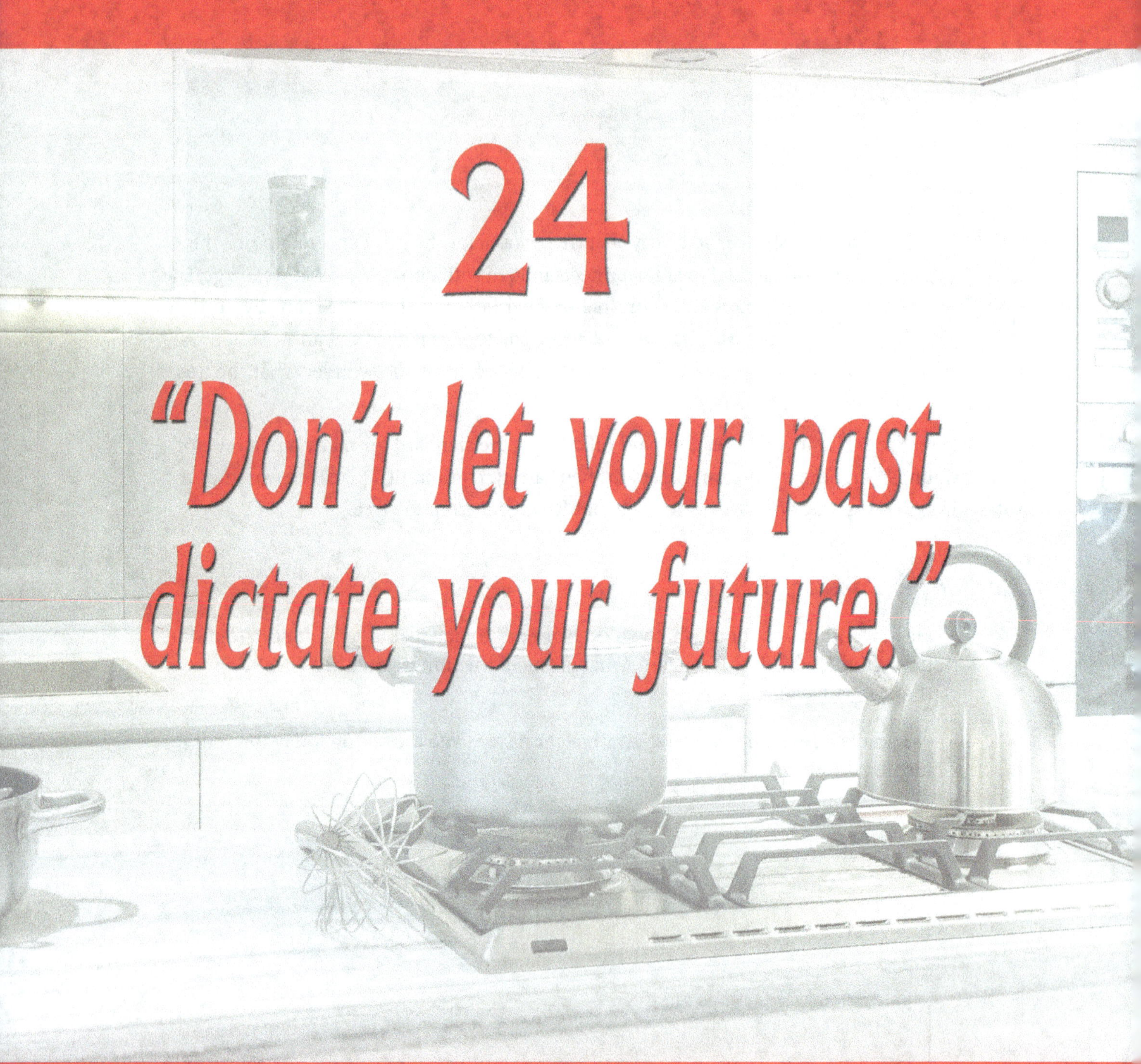

24
"Don't let your past dictate your future."

I loved me some Aunt Flossie. Just to sit and visit with her was a gift. She would have me laughing so hard sometimes I would cry. When she first moved to town, I loved going to her house. It was spacious and spotless. I can't recall a time there wasn't a pot on the stove. The aroma reminded me of that good old down-home cooking. I didn't like to eat much, but she made a believer out of me. Her crackling bread was even better than mama's, and that's saying something! Almost hands down, Mary Jane was the best cook in town!

I marveled at how Aunt Flossie settled her family into their new home. It was so different than what they had left behind when they moved north. As children, we would always go to see them when we went to Mississippi. Their home was spotless, the food was great, and they worked hard to keep it together. Sharecropping was not the ideal employment situation.

I was excited when their family moved and came to town. Over the years, as my cousins got jobs and had children, I have felt her determination and legacy. Now her children own multiple properties and businesses. Their children are following in the same pathway and have become pillars in the community, not just with their businesses, but with their gifts and commitment to the community.

Questions to Consider

What can you recall that has challenged you?

Did you overcome it? If yes, how so?

What did you inherit from previous generations? How has it helped you? How did it hinder you?

25
"You cain't always let the left hand know what the right hand doin'."
10TH

Mama was a financial genius. She and Daddy were the stable forces. Mama kept a sock in her bosom. As a young girl, I wondered why. I wasn't by myself; my other sisters talked about the sock filled with money, too. Finally, I had the courage and the nerve to ask.

"Mama, why you keep that sock up there?"

"Bob Ann, you just too nosy. But I'll tell you this, when we short of money, I can always make up the difference."

I thought about it some more. The next day as we were cooking, I had to go back to the conversation about the sock.

"Mama, where your sock at? I don't see it."

"That ain't none of your business. Always asking questions. That sock is my business for this house business, and it ain't nobody's business but mine."

"Daddy don't know?" I asked. She cut her eyes at me. I knew I had crossed the line. I didn't ask no more questions.

Questions to Consider

Are there things you do quietly to help others?

If yes, why do you do it quietly?

26

"Don't worry
'bout the mule goin' blind.
Jes' get in the wagon
and shake the line."

Her mind was in a whirl as she scratched Mama Saddler's head.

"Now scratch it hard in that spot. It is really itching. I'm so glad you came up to wash my head."

"Now you know I will do anything you ask me. So, I don't mind coming up to help you out," I said.

"What Jane doin' today? And where that baby at?" she asked.

"Well, Mama is baking pies, and Shaun is right there with her," I said. We laughed and talked about the two of them and how proud Daddy was of that baby.

"Now what's on your mind? You goin' in and out of the conversation like you carryin' a heavy load."

"Oh, nothing," I said. "I'm just trying to figure out how I will pay for college, take care of Shaun, finish this 20-semester hours of classes, and work my three jobs."

"Well, look like you in the school, you taking the classes, you passing them, and the baby is doing fine. What I tell you before? Gone, girl! Jes' shake the line!"

Questions to Consider

How do you respond when there is an obstacle or an unclear path for you to take?

Do you internalize it, write a plan, and/or talk about it with someone?

Which do you do, and why?

27

"A lil' sugar
go' a long ways."

Walking into the office of Mr. Bertrum always came with a feeling of dread. He had been known to talk very little, but he always carried a big stick. Janice said she was called into his office, and it wasn't a pretty sight. She said he called her parents, and they were in the office when she walked in. Everything she thought she had done without Mr. Bertrum knowing was brought out in the meeting with her and her parents. Janice was put on probation for six months.

I had recently been in the lunchroom talking with Jimmy. He was in the same grade as me. We were in different homerooms but had two classes together. Jimmy was a loner and rarely talked to anyone. I like Jimmy and enjoyed our brief conversations. There was a group of popular kids who thought they were the sauce. I just looked at them and shook my head as they walked by pointing and snickering. It was then that I saw Mr. Bertrum staring at me and Jimmy.

So now, a week later, I was being called into his office. What could it be? I could hear talking. I knocked and announced myself.

"Come in, Brittney," said Mr. Bertrum. When I opened the door, I was surpised to see my parents, Jimmy and his parents, and a bunch of balloons tied to a large box. I had to catch my breath.

Questions to Consider

How would you have reacted to the request to go to Mr. Bertrum's office? Why?

What struck you about the conversation with Jimmy?

Have your ever felt like Jimmy? If so, when?

What characteristics do you think Brittney has? Do you see yourself having any of those traits?

How might they serve you on your life journey?

28

"Crazy as a Bessie-bug."

Zeke the electrician was an alcoholic genius. He was known as the town drunk. I could never understand why my dad would call him when there was electrical work to be done. I could see him turning the corner from 4th Street and walking toward the house.

"Daddy, here comes Zeke!" shouted Katherine.

Whistling as he walked, Daddy sauntered from the kitchen and out to the porch.

"Hey, Simpson, what you need?" Zeke asked as he walked up the steps and onto the porch.

"Well, look like I got a short in the light switch goin' up the stairs, and I need you to look at the electrical box 'cause the lights keep goin' off," Daddy said.

"Aw 'ight, I got my tools and my stuff," Zeke said. As he always did, he began to sing and do a jig and then talk to himself, mumbling, smiling, and laughing all at the same time.

I thought to myself, *How could Daddy have so much faith in this man.* But Zeke did the work, which spoke for itself, in what seemed to me was a crazy state of mind. No matter the day of the week or the time of day, Zeke was always himself. Anyone could see and feel his pain, but he presented himself happy and never said a mumbling word that was out of line.

Questions to Consider

When have you seen someone and judged his or her ability to get the job done?

What did you see that led you to some type of judgment or bias? Did it hold true?

Have you ever stopped to think about how people present themselves?

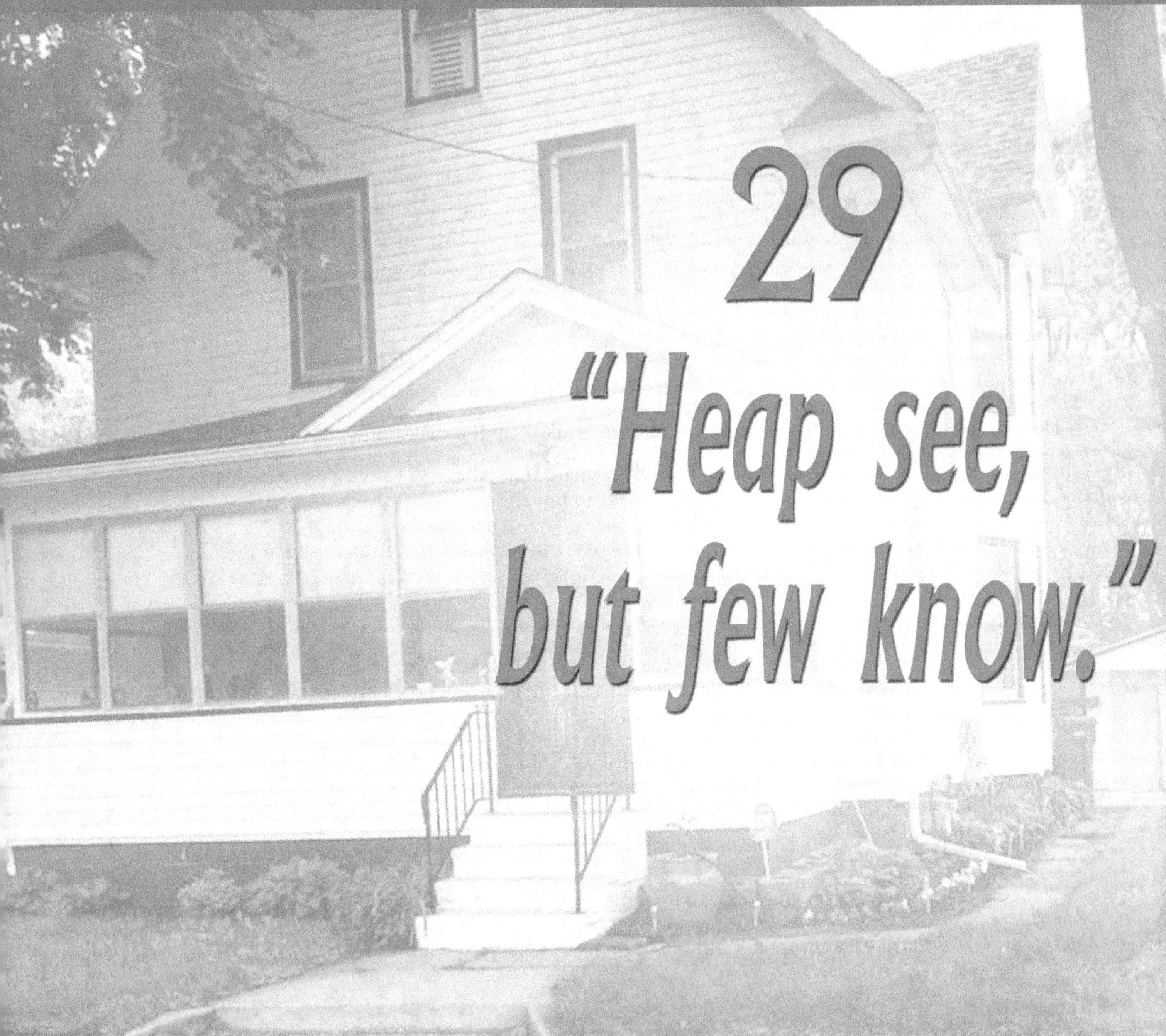

29
"Heap see,
but few know."

30
"The leanin' tree
ain't always the first one to fall."

Eleven kids, people coming for every meal—all them gals—and Dub the only one working at a job. Worked at the plant, and here he done went and bought a big house in the white folks' neighborhood.

"He'll never pay for that house," Jessie said.

"I know," Splo said.

The townfolks often questioned how Dub and Jane were making ends meet. Jessie and Splo worked at the same plant with Dub. They knew how far their dollars stretched, and they didn't have near 'bout the number of mouths to feed.

Not only were they livin' in a big house, but it was a revolving door. People came in the front and went out the back all day long. As people went by the house, they would comment and wonder what was happenin' in that house. They'd been feeding the hobos, renting rooms to families migrating to the North, and hosting big dinners for family members and friends. There were unspoken rules everybody knew. Over the years, it had become known as the safe house and the praying house. And most of those 11 kids turned out to be just like Dub and Jane.

Questions to Consider

What do you think was happening with the couple?

Why do you imagine people from all walks of life came to them?

How do you envision the mental and material resource needed to sustain their hospitality?

"My, my, my," Geraldine said. She looked across the street at Dub and Jane's house. They had a house full of children. All those girls, two small boys, and dogs, and Dub was the only one workin'.

"I don't know what they gone do with all them chirins. Jane havin' a baby every year. And all them people they feed."

Geraldine and George had only two children, George Jr. and Carolyn. They could get their children everything and anything they wanted. Mr. George, would come across the street smoking his big cigar, bragging about the money, cars, clothes, and all the things his children had and how good life was.

Over the years, Dub and Jane's children grew up, and some of them left home, but they came back home for every holiday, sent gifts, fixed the house, and celebrated their parents on any and all occasions. Each time the kids came home, Geraldine and George were invited over to share in the celebration of food, fun, laughter, stories, singing, and dancing. But Geraldine and George rarely saw their two kids, Carolyn and George Jr. They had their own lives to live, and they did. You could see the sadness in Geraldine's and George's eyes and feel the pain in their voices.

Questions to Consider

Do you think that having more is better? Why or why not?

When have you judged someone based on what you see?

What did you learn?